The clouds broke up and a pale
love to stay here all night with you," he said, "but it is growing late and you must work tomorrow. We don't want to jeopardize your job in the mansion."

"Please. Can I go with you, my darling? I only want to be with you. My parents are still urging me to change my mind and marry Antony. Please take me with you."

"I wish it could be," he said, "but it is too risky. There are too many dangers; snakes, alligators, and wild animals. And if Turnbull's people happen to find us, it will be more difficult for two of us to elude them. If they caught us, we both would be whipped and chained. Be patient and pray, and maybe your parents will change their mind. Now we must worry about getting the new governor's help. Go back before you are missed."

"I don't know when I will find another opportunity to come here," she said. "How can we meet again?"

"There won't be many opportunities, and we must accept that. I can't expect Chucuraha to be around whenever I want him. When he makes another visit to trade, I'm hoping Father Camps will contact him. We must depend on those two, and that will be chancy."

After a passionate goodbye, he watched her go until she disappeared behind a building. As he turned to leave, he heard a male voice.

"You there. What are you doing out here?"

He recognized the voice. It was Louis Bruno, a Corporal with a brutal reputation--the one who had the young boy stoned.

Anita's voice came in reply. "I couldn't sleep, and was taking a walk."

"Wait. I know you. You're the Usina girl…Anita. They say you are chummy with Miguel…you meeting him out here?"

Miguel started moving toward the sound of their voices.

"No. I don't know what you're talking about."

"I don't believe you. Good thing Turnbull has us doing night patrols. He thinks Miguel might be alive and hiding near here."

"No…no. I'm just walking because I can't sleep."

"Alright. I won't say anything about this if we can have a little fun

1

together."

"No. Please. Let me go."

Miguel rounded the corner of the building and saw Anita struggling with Bruno. He Ran toward them, and Bruno turned when he heard the sound of his footsteps. Bruno's mouth flew open and he fumbled for the pistol on his belt. But Miguel was quicker as he lunged forward with his knife. It was over in a matter of seconds. Bruno lay still on the ground, mortally wounded by a stab in the heart.

Anita gasped, but she was not alarmed, for she had seen death many times in the fields. "What are we going to do now?"

"Go back to the mansion and forget what you have seen. I'll figure out what to do with the body."

~ ~ * ~ ~

THE MINORCANS OF FLORIDA

A Story of White Slavery

By Donald H Sullivan

Copyright 2011 Donald H Sullivan

All Rights Reserved

ISBN: 978-0-557-09155-3

Revised edition, originally titled *The Menorcans of Florida*

    This is a work of fiction inspired by a historical event. Most of the events recounted in the story are based on the testimonies of colonists during Governor Tonyn's investigation of Dr. Turnbull's alleged abuses of his indentured servants at the New Smyrna Colony.
    All characters in the story are fictitious except those in the following list.

Dr. Andrew Turnbull
Gov. James Grant
Gov. Patrick Tonyn
Father Pedro Camps
Father Bartolommeo Casanovas
Ramon Rogero
Francisco Pelicer

    The roles and dialogues of the above characters are purely speculative, but the story endeavors to characterize them in the way that history has portrayed them.
    The last two, Ramon and Francisco, took a huge risk by escaping Turnbull's colony, making their way to St. Augustine, and notifying Gov. Tonyn of the plight of the colonists.
    The fictitious characters, such as Turnbull's overseers, slave drivers, and colonists, are based on the actual people who made up Turnbull's colony. Other than those, any resemblance to persons, living or dead, is strictly coincidental.

FOREWORD

The British acquired Florida from Spain in 1763 due to a war between the two countries in the mid 1700s, giving them a new colony. In hopes of populating the territory, Britain granted large tracts of land to certain individuals One of those individuals was Dr. Andrew Turnbull, a wealthy Scotsman.

Turnbull was enticed by the possibility of wealth and power. He recruited and transported over 1,000 people from the Mediterranean area to colonize the land that he called New Smyrna (named after the homeland of his wife.) He had planned on less than half that number, between three and four hundred, but due to an ongoing famine in Minorca, a large number of people from that island volunteered.

It was the largest single group sent to colonize land in the New World up to that time. The New Smyrna Colony covered over 100,000 acres and was nearly three times the size of the colony at Jamestown.

~ ~ * ~ ~

Eight ships, chartered by Dr. Turnbull, left the port of Mahon, Minorca in mid-April 1768. The ships were bound for Florida, carrying a total of 1,403 passengers, all of whom were indentured servants of Turnbull. He intended to use these indentured servants to work his plantations in Florida and to colonize the 100,000 acres of land granted to him by the British government. In return, he promised to free the servants and give them plots of land when their term of servitude expired.

The ships began arriving in Florida in June 1768, with the last one arriving in mid-July. Of the 1,403 passengers, only 1,255 survived, an indication of the terrible conditions aboard the ships during the voyage.

Upon arrival in Florida, the colonists became no better than slaves. Large numbers of them died because of brutal treatment, diseases, and harsh living conditions in the colony. Turnbull refused to release them and give them their promised plots of land when their term of indenture expired.

He claimed that the term of indenture did not start until the servant had worked to pay off travel expenses from Minorca to

Florida.

However, the Minorcans claimed that Turnbull had promised them free transportation to Florida.

~ ~ * ~ ~

The Minorcans of Florida

May 23, 1768. Miguel Ortegas watched as the body of his father was released into the sea. He scarcely heard the words that Father Casanovas uttered as the body was committed to the deep. He was in a daze; everything around him seemed like a dream. He had cried until he could cry no more. His emotions were drained dry.

He stood on the deck, barely aware when friends of his father expressed their condolences. Of the nearly two hundred people on the ship, many of them knew his father, who had been a carpenter. He had done work for hundreds of people in Minorca.

He remembered many times when his father refused payment for small jobs like door or window repair when he knew that people had no money to spare.

His father had observed his forty-third birthday aboard the ship just one week before he died. The ship had been at sea for over two months of what was supposed to have been but a six week voyage. But rough seas and storms had blown them off course several times.

Food was running low and spoiling, and nearly every passenger had sickened, including Miguel. His father had been one of twenty-three on the ship who had died from food poisoning, scurvy, or unknown causes.

At age fifteen, he was now alone. His mother had died when he was nine. He had an older brother, Roberto, who chose to stay in Minorca, as he had just married and had a good job working for a shipping company.

After the funeral he returned to his hammock in the crowded compartment, which was quarters for single men. The hammocks were a 3x6 foot piece of canvas, held tightly between beams by four ropes, one at each corner. His father's hammock, now empty, was directly above his.

The space between decks in the compartment was less than five feet, and even Miguel, at five-feet-two, had to stoop when walking through.

Directly across the aisle from Miguel was Jose Reyes. He liked Jose, although the man was simple-minded and sometimes spouted nonsense. But at times he could be rational, and when so he was good company. He was a tall, skinny bachelor of about thirty-five. He had no relatives aboard, but claimed that he had some on one of the seven other Florida-bound ships carrying colonists to the British colony of New Smyrna.

On the hammock above Jose was Giuseppe Pasquale. He was a swarthy Italian with a thin mustache who had a perpetually annoyed look on his face. He frequently snored, mumbled in his sleep, and broke wind. The latter being the reason that Giuseppe and Jose frequently had words.

The ship was in fairly calm waters now, and it was smooth sailing. It was quiet in the compartment. Some were playing cards, some were talking in low voices, and some were sleeping. Miguel was glad for the smooth sailing. Rough seas didn't make him seasick, but it made many of the others sick. Their gagging, puking, and moaning made life miserable for all. There was a perpetual stink in the compartment from the vomit.

He lay there on his hammock, staring up at the empty hammock above him. He remembered how excited his father had been when Dr. Andrew Turnbull came to Minorca looking for volunteers willing to go to Florida and work his plantations.

At the time, Minorca was in a three-year drought that had caused a severe famine on the island, so Turnbull was able to pick up many volunteers there. He had already recruited a number of Italian and Greek volunteers, but Minorcans far outnumbered both of those combined.

Turnbull came promising volunteers free passage to Florida plus quarters and provisions at Turnbull's colony. In exchange, the colonists were required to sign a contract of indenture to work Turnbull's plantations for a specified term. After the term was up, they were promised their freedom and a large plot of land.

Miguel's father was lured by the promise of such a large tract of land. Turnbull was especially looking for tradesmen like carpenters and masons, and as an inducement he offered a short three-year term of indenture instead of the seven year term for laborers.

His father gladly signed, but on condition that Miguel be signed as a carpenter's apprentice. He had at first requested that Miguel be signed as a first class carpenter, but Turnbull hesitated.

"At fifteen, he is too young to sign as a tradesman. I'll agree to sign him up as an apprentice until he turns eighteen."

"I know that he can do carpentry," said his father, "but I understand your concerns so I'll accept your terms. Agreed"

The word quickly spread among the people of Minorca that Dr. Turnbull was a wealthy Scotsman who had been granted a hundred thousand acres of land in East Florida by the British Crown, and that he was establishing a colony on the land. He planned on planting fields of indigo, sugar cane, and olives, which would reap great profits.

The man is already wealthy and dreams of even more wealth. All poor Papa dreamed of was working out his indenture and getting his own plot of land. Like a thousand other Minorcans, Miguel's father was lured by the promise of his own plot of land and a new life in America.

Turnbull had planned on recruiting four hundred people from around the Mediterranean area, but ended up signing far more than he had planned on. So many, in fact, that he needed to charter eight ships for the voyage. Miguel had heard that the total number of colonists was over fourteen hundred.

Miguel's thoughts were suddenly interrupted.

"I'm going to shoot him," shouted Jose.

A few of the men looked up from their card game, then went back to their playing.

."What are you talking about," Miguel said. "Shoot who?"

"Turnbull, that's who. Because of him you've lost your father. And there are many others who have died since we left Minorca. They would still be alive if Turnbull hadn't come."

Jose lapsed into mumbling angrily, and Miguel closed his eyes in thought.

He's right. Papa would still be alive if Turnbull hadn't come. But I must remember, too, that we chose to come. Papa and I signed an indenture agreement for three years. And, too, it's not Turnbull's fault that we were blown off course several times.

Jose reached over and shook him. "Miguel, did you hear me?"

"Sorry, I must have dozed off. What were you saying?"

"I'm going to cut his throat. Will you help me?"

"Forget it, Jose. They would hang the both of us."

There was a long moment of silence, when the only sound was Giuseppe's snoring and the murmur of conversation in the compartment.

Finally, Jose whispered, "Yes, I guess you're right." He went back to his mumbling.

~ ~ * ~ ~

July 11, 1768. The ship arrived in St. Augustine, Florida, nearly three months after leaving Port Mahon, Minorca.

Before debarking, Miguel picked up his father's canvas bag that held all their belongings and slung the strap over his shoulder. The rest of their belongings were left in the care of his older brother in Minorca.

Miguel learned that the other seven ships had already arrived. Most of the passengers of the other ships had already left St. Augustine for the New Smyrna colony. Some went by sea and some went by land. The land route was a seventy-five mile walk on the recently completed King's Road, which had been built over an old Indian trail..

If we have to walk for seventy-five miles, I can't do it carrying my bag. I'll probably have to leave most of my stuff here.

After debarking, the travelers were gathered into an open field in the north part of the city near the old Spanish fort. In an agreement with Turnbull, Governor Grant had arranged to provide food and lodging to the transient travelers.

The group was given portions of peas, potatoes, salt beef, and cabbage. There was also choices of mullet, turnips cooked with salt pork, and fresh bread. Miguel wolfed down the meal, the best he had since leaving Minorca.

As he finished his meal, a pretty girl, about his age, approached. Her features were delicate with large brown eyes, and she had an olive complexion, as did many Minorcans. He didn't know her, but had seen her on the ship a few times. He was surprised when she stopped. She seemed embarrassed.

"Are...are you Miguel Ortegas?"

He smiled at her. "Yes, I am."

"My name is Anita Usina. I was on the same ship with you, but we were in different quarters. I saw you at your father's funeral, and I just want to say I'm sorry. I hope you are doing well."

"Thank you. I am doing fine now."

"I heard that altogether nearly two-hundred passengers died," she said "They say that some of the ships we were on have carried slaves from Africa." She paused. "Do you have relatives here?"

"No, but I will be alright. My papa made Turnbull agree to take me as a carpenter's apprentice as a condition of his signing for three years. Turnbull needed carpenters, so he agreed."

"We got an agreement from Turnbull, too," she said. "My papa signed on as a blacksmith and Mama and me will work the fields. Turnbull agreed that our servitude will be for only three years, the same as Papa's, and not the seven years for field workers. Where are you from?"

"I am from a community near Ciudadela. And you?"

"We are from Mahon."

"Anita, Anita, where are you?" A male voice shouted.

"That's Papa," she said "I have to go."

He smiled as he watched her go. *I like her. Just a few words with her made me feel a lot better. I hope we can meet again.*

~ ~ * ~ ~

Felipe Usina signed on with Turnbull as a blacksmith. His trade had been rather prosperous in Minorca until the drought plagued the whole island. He was not a farmer, but he depended to a large degree on the farmers for business. As the drought dragged on seemingly without end, he saw the chance to sign on with Turnbull as a blessing.

He would be bound to a contract for only three years, after which he would become a landowner in the British colony of East Florida. He would continue his blacksmith trade, but being a landowner would gain him higher position and privileges.

   He smiled and hugged his daughter. "Where have you been, Anita? I've been looking all over for you. Your mama and I have been worried."

   "I'm sorry, Papa. I didn't mean to worry you and Mama. I was talking to Miguel Ortegas, the boy who lost his Papa during the voyage. It's so sad. He is an orphan and all alone now."

   "Yes, it is very sad. From what I hear, though, he learned the carpenter trade from his father and has a tradesman contract with Turnbull. He will be alright, so we needn't be too concerned."

   "He's very nice, papa. I talked to him for only a few minutes, but I like him very much."

   At this point her mother came up. She giggled. "You like who very much, sweet?"

   "I was telling Papa about my meeting Miguel Ortegas. I do like him, and I think he likes me."

   Carmen looked puzzled for a moment, then nodded. "Oh yes, the one who is orphaned now. It's easy for a girl to be attracted to a boy in such tragic circumstances. I'm glad that you are concerned, but I urge you not to let it go farther than that. You must always remember that you are betrothed to Antony."

   Antony Capo. I wish I weren't betrothed to him. He's a nice man, but he's twenty years old. Besides, the betrothal was arranged by an agreement with Antony's parents and my parents.

   ~ ~ * ~ ~

   Miguel was not on the list to go by sea to New Smyrna, he would be with the group that walked. But he was relieved to learn that Governor Grant had furnished the walkers with several horse drawn wagons to carry their belongings.

   The march from St. Augustine to New Smyrna took a little over three days. They walked at a normal pace, stopping for a few short breaks each day, and allowing six or seven hours each night for sleep.

There was thunderstorm on the afternoon of the first day, and it rained nearly every day of the trip.
. He looked for Anita, but did not see her during the entire march.

~ ~ * ~ ~

Anita and her family boarded the ship for the trip south to Turnbull's colony. It was better than walking, but she did not look forward to being tossed about by the heaving seas. But the ship never reached the open sea; it followed an inland waterway, a route between a series of islands and the mainland. It was a very smooth ride.

The ship was not as crowded as the ship that she boarded in Minorca, and the trip was pleasant, lasting less than a day.

Anita looked for, but did not see Miguel during the trip.

~ ~ * ~ ~

Miguel, like everyone else, was disheartened by the conditions the colonists found at Turnbull's colony. Turnbull had led them to believe that the land had already been cleared by African slaves. However, they learned that the ship bringing the slaves from Africa sank at sea, leaving no survivors.

Housing was supposed to be available for all the colonists upon arrival. Food would be plentiful, they were told, and clothing and shoes would be furnished to the colonists.

Instead, they found that none of the land had been cleared, and that the colonists would be expected to clear hundreds of acres. The only housing awaiting them was thatched palmetto huts, built by a few African slaves that Turnbull had purchased from plantation owners in South Carolina and brought down to his Florida colony. There were not nearly enough huts to accommodate everyone. And the Florida heat was smothering.

Food and provisions had been stored for an expected four hundred colonists, not nearly enough for the more than twelve hundred that arrived. Turnbull had anticipated about four hundred recruits from the Mediterranean area, mostly Italian and Greek.

But due to the drought conditions in Minorca, he picked up over nine hundred recruits from that island. Turnbull turned down none of the recruits, but he had not laid on more provisions to accommodate them. There would be severe rationing until more provisions arrived from St. Augustine and Charleston.

There were only a dozen African slaves available that Turnbull had brought from South Carolina. In addition, there were ten more Africans, but they weren't workers; they had been slave drivers on a cotton plantation . Turnbull wanted experienced drivers--he called them his corporals--to push the workers in his labor force, and those ten Africans he judged to be experienced and well suited for the task.

Turnbull also had a number of overseers, who were English and also from a cotton plantation in South Carolina. All the overseers were experienced as supervisors of African slaves. The chief overseer was named Carlton Clay, a big, ruddy-faced redhead. He wore a wide brimmed felt hat with the brim curled up on one side.

There was resentment among the colonists. They did not like it that their overseers were formerly supervising slaves, nor did they like it that Turnbull was using his slave drivers to push them. They were supposed to be indentured servants, not slaves.

Before the new colonists had a chance to rest from their trip, Clay was making up work assignments for them. Some would be cutters, sawing and chopping trees and brush. Some would be digging roots, removing stumps, and burning brush. Also, he made a list of workers who would build more thatched huts. The Africans, who had learned how to make thatched huts from the local Indians, made the existing huts and would show the colonists how to make them.

Miguel learned that he was to be a stump remover. He waved his hands and got Clay's attention.

"What do you want, boy."

"Sir, I was signed on as a carpenter. Shouldn't I be assigned to do carpenter work?"

Clay called him forward. "What is your name?"

"Miguel Ortegas."

Clay checked his list. "My list shows you as a carpenter's apprentice, not a carpenter. But that does not matter. Starting tomorrow carpenters, blacksmiths, and other tradesmen will work at clearing until they are needed to work in their trade."

"Yes sir." Miguel turned to go.

Clay caught his arm. "Just a minute, boy. Mr. Miller, our chief carpenter, wants good carpenters, not trainees. He already has about twenty first class carpenters ready to start building. If he needs laborers to help his carpenters and masons, he can draw all he needs from our workforce.

"I'm going to make up new papers for you to sign, and then Dr. Turnbull will sign them. Your old contract will be voided, and you will be better used as a laborer in the fields with seven years indenture."

"But sir, I can do first class carpentry. All the carpenters I've worked with say so. If you will give me a chance..."

"That will be enough. Now shut up or I'll send you to the whipping post."

Clay dismissed him and continued addressing the new colonists.

"I want to remind all of you that Dr. Turnbull is the law in this colony. As long as you keep the rules and do your work you will be alright. That's all I have for now. Breakfast will be at first light. I want everybody gathered here right after breakfast tomorrow morning. Now you may get ready for supper."

The crowd broke up, and everyone was pulling their cups and bowls from their bags and trunks. They lined up for a small serving of corn gruel and hardtack bread, prepared and served by a African slaves and several Minorcans who had volunteered as cooks.

Miguel was outraged. *I'm not going to take this. First chance I get, I'll run away. I'll go to St. Augustine and then stowaway on a ship to Minorca. I'm not going to stay here, nor will I sign any more papers.*

~ ~ * ~ ~

The few thatched huts that were available were assigned to the colonists with tradesmen having first priority. Anita was disappointed with the hut assigned to her father. It was devoid of furnishings save for a couple of wooden crates and what few belongings they had placed in the hut. One candle was issued per hut, but her mother had brought along several candles in their belongings.

The huts were spaced far apart with all facing the river. The days were hot, but nights were mostly cooled from breezes off the ocean.

There was only one room in their hut, but Anita's father had rigged a blanket as a screen to partition a small place to give her some privacy.

"I heard today that Miguel's contract was voided, and that he would now be indentured for seven years as a farmer. I am angry. With all that he has endured, he now faces more hardships."

"Yes," her mother agreed, "It does seem an injustice. But he is young, and in seven years he will still be a young man in his twenties. He will become a landowner then, and few people of his age have such standing." Carmen hugged her daughter. "Don't worry over it, Sweet. We are having hardships enough of our own."

But she did worry, and fell into a fretful sleep thinking of Miguel.

~ ~ * ~ ~

That night, all those who were not assigned a hut had to sleep in the open. Miguel estimated there were seven or eight hundred, including himself. Everyone chose to sleep on the sandy bank of the river, careful to stay above the high tide mark, and hope the weather stayed clear.

What they called a river was actually a lagoon, or run of salt water between the mainland and a chain of offshore islands. This stretch of the river was wide but shallow. The inland waterway went northward all the way to St. Augustine and beyond. The waterfront of the colony ran along the river bank for a distance of several miles.

Miguel found a blanket in his bag and spread it on the sand. As he lay there, he looked up to see that someone was spreading a blanket next to his. It was Jose.

"Hello, Jose, good to see you."

"Good to see you, too, and I'm glad that I don't have to put up with Giuseppe anymore. I saw you when you talked to Clay today. I thought he would have you whipped. I don't like it here. I want to go home."

Miguel was glad to see that Jose was not in one of his loony moods

He lowered his voice. "I'm not going to stay here and take this, Jose. He actually threatened to have me whipped, like a slave."

"What are you going to do?"

"Go to St. Augustine and stowaway on a boat to Europe, and then go to Minorca."

"I'll go with you. We can go by King's Road because we know that way and won't get lost."

"No. That will be the first place they look for us."

"Then how will we go?"

"They say there's a big swamp behind the colony," said Miguel. We'll go through the swamp; they won't expect us to leave that way. We can circle around the colony and come out by the river. We can make a raft from tree branches and follow the river to St. Augustine."

~ ~ * ~ ~

Miguel and Jose started out before daylight the next morning. They carried their heavy travel bags a short way into the swamp, then decided they were too heavy and hid them. Miguel pulled a hatchet and a coil of rope from his bag, as he would need those items to make a raft.

They slogged their way through the muck and mire of the swamp until they came to the bank of a creek. They eyed the stream, about fifteen feet wide. The water was like tea, darkened by the decaying leaves.

"It doesn't look too wide," said Jose. "Maybe it's shallow enough to wade across."

"We can swim it..." Miguel stopped in mid sentence. A big alligator moved on the opposite bank, then slid into the creek. Jose gasped and stepped back as the reptile disappeared into the murky water.

Miguel laid his hand on Jose's shoulder. "Don't be afraid," he said. "It's only an alligator, and there are many of them in Florida. I heard some people on the ship talking about them and they said that they won't hurt you if you don't bother them.

"All the same," he said, " we better not cross here. We'd better follow along the bank until we find a way to cross. Sooner or later there's bound to be a spot shallow enough to wade across."

Miguel didn't like it. He had heard there were alligators in Florida, but never expected to see one. He was beginning to have thoughts about turning back to Turnbull's colony. He probably would have turned back already had it not been for Jose. When they left before dawn, Miguel had already changed his mind after going a short way. Stowing away on a ship was beginning to look more and more like a hare-brained idea.

17

But Jose refused to turn back. "I'm going by myself if you don't go."

"It's still early," Miguel argued. "Maybe they haven't missed us yet."

"Ha. I'll bet they're probably looking for us right now."

Miguel tried to argue, but couldn't persuade Jose to turn back. He did not want to abandon his friend, and reluctantly agreed to continue.

"Wait," said Jose. "We don't have to look for a better spot. I'll kill that alligator so we can cross." With that, Jose made a growling sound and showed his teeth.

Oh no. He's going into one of his loony moods. I sure don't need that now.

"How do you think you'll kill that alligator?

"I'll just jump in there with my knife and stab it to death."

"It might kill you, and then what would I do? And what if there is more than one? Let's go and look for a good place to cross, and we'll both make it."

"I guess you're right," said Jose, "but let's rest a while before we start." He sat down on a fallen log. Miguel started to sit down next to his companion when he noticed a movement under the log where Jose was seated. He gasped. It was a huge snake. He opened his mouth to warn Jose, but it was too late.

The snake struck and Jose cried out in pain. He jumped up as the snake slithered into the creek. He rolled up his trousers to reveal two puncture wounds on the back of his leg, just below the knee. The area of the bite mark was already darkening and beginning to swell.

Miguel was horrified. "My God! We'd better hurry back to the colony for help."

Amazingly, Jose was calm. "They say that if you are bitten by a snake, you are supposed to keep quiet so that the poison will work slow…and maybe weaken. I better stay here, while you go back for help."

The normally slow-witted Jose was keeping his wits under a terrifying situation. Miguel could think of no alternative to Jose's suggestion.. "Alright," he said. "We've only been gone about three hours. If I hurry there's plenty of time."

Jose nodded, then lapsed into mumbling. He began to giggle at some secret joke, and seemed unaware of Miguel leaving.

There were no appreciable landmarks to follow, but Miguel had a good sense of direction, and set out confidently. It was only mid morning and the sun was still low, so there would be plenty of time to get help, and to get Jose back before dark.

It was stupid of me to have such an idea to begin with, and it was stupid of me to listen to Jose and refuse to turn back when we had a chance. Maybe they wouldn't yet have missed us. How could we expect to survive in a wilderness that we knew nothing about?

On top of that we had no weapons or food. They'll probably punish me, but I'll just have to take it. They'll punish poor Jose, too, if he survives the snake bite.

The thought of Jose waiting and in danger of dying made Miguel speed up his pace. It was only mid morning, but already hot and humid.

Turnbull told us that the climate here was about the same as in Minorca. He lied. It never got this hot and muggy.

He looked up at the Spanish moss hanging from the tree branches, giving the swamp a gloomy look. He wished he were back in Minorca where they had no alligators to worry about. *In all my fifteen years of growing up in Minorca and roaming the island, I never saw creatures like alligators.*

Miguel left the swamp and reached dry land. He should reach the settlement soon. From the corner of his eye he saw a group of several men to his left. One of the men yelled. Miguel heard the sharp crack of a pistol and felt a sting on his upper right arm. He stopped and raised his arms in surrender.

As the men approached, he could see that none of them were Minorcans, Italians, or any other group that came on the ships. There were two men who appeared to be British and one African. He later learned the two whites were overseers, a short, stocky, blonde-bearded man named McCormick, and a slim but sinewy man named Grey. The tall, angular African was a driver called Corporal Silas. Grey carried a pistol, which he reloaded and stuck in his belt. One of the men spoke some Spanish and asked where the other escapee was hiding. Miguel, like most Minorcans, spoke Catalan. He figured that his English was as good or better than the man's Spanish, so he answered in English, and explained what happened. The men took him to Clay.

"I'll send one of the corporals with you tomorrow morning," said Clay. In the meantime, join the group you're assigned to and go to work. I'll leave word with Carver, your overseer, to mete out the punishment that he sees fit." He paused. "And he'll send you to my office after work tonight to sign your new indenture agreement."

"But there's still time to go get Jose and be back before sundown," Miguel protested . "He may die before morning."

"Serve him right," said Silas. "We outta let him rot in the swamp."

Clay nodded. "Tomorrow morning is the earliest I'll send anybody. I'll not risk any of my people being in the swamp with them snakes and gators after dark."

Miguel's arm was only grazed by the bullet, and the wound had already stopped bleeding. But it was still painful, and he reached up with his left hand to feel for bleeding.

Clay snorted. "A little scratch. Now get to work."

~ ~ * ~ ~

Anita had rarely seen her father in such a foul mood before.

He frowned. "Turnbull is not keeping his agreement," he said, "but there is nothing we can do about it. I and the other tradesmen, like carpenters and masons, were supposed to work in our trades. Now he tells us that we must work in the fields until the land is cleared. Who knows how long that will take?"

"He is the supreme law here," said Carmen. "What can we do? We can't run away. The surrounding woods are full of gators, snakes, panthers, and bears. Besides, they say there are wild Indians out there."

"Yes, said Felipe, and all of Turnbull's overseers are armed."

Felipe pulled his wife and daughter close and hugged them. "Turnbull also promised that you two would do only farming chores, not hard work like clearing land."

"But they say that the slaves who were supposed to do the clearing all died when their ship sank." said Carmen. "It's not all Turnbull's fault."

"Maybe not," said Felipe. "But it is we who have become the

slaves. We are forced to do as he says. We have overseers and slave drivers over us. We have meager rations. One of the slaves from South Carolina told us that the slaves on the cotton plantations eat better than we do and live in better quarters."

Mama was right, thought Anita, *we are having troubles enough of our own. But I still think about poor Miguel.*

~ ~ * ~ ~

Miguel reported to Carver, a paunchy man sporting a wide mustache and a goatee. The overseer looked him over. "You're pretty skinny and frail looking for this kind of work, boy," he said, "but you better do your share or I'll take it out of your hide." He guffawed. "Clay sent word that you was a runaway, and left it to me to judge the punishment, because my crew is the one that suffered the loss of your labor.

"I'm a pretty lenient man compared to some here, so since you came back on your own you'll only get forty lashes. Consider yourself lucky."

A squat, heavy set African named Corporal Jacob led him to a pine tree that served as their whipping post.

"Take your shirt off, boy, and hug the tree," Jacob ordered.

Miguel did as he was told. Jacob tied his hands together, and administered the lashes as Carver watched. Miguel didn't know what Jacob used as a whip, but it was like fire with each lash. Just when Miguel thought he couldn't take any more, Jacob released him and turned him over to Carver.

"You're lucky on all counts, boy, Jacob is one of the easy ones. If it had been Silas, he'd have brought blood."

His back still painful, Miguel joined the stump removal crew, who were equipped with shovels, axes, and mattocks. He noticed that boys and girls even younger than he were working. The overseers claimed that Turnbull wanted every hand busy until the land was cleared.

Smaller kids were used to bring water to the workers. The well water was tepid and had an earthy odor. Miguel saw several people collapse from exhaustion. They were permitted a short "water break," after which a driver would force them back to work.

After work, he was on his way to Clay's office when he met a small group who knew his father. He stopped and answered questions about the wound on his arm and his attempted escape in the swamp.

The Usinas were nearby, and Anita came over.

"Mama brought some ointment from Minorca," she said. "Let me put some on your wound and bandage it."

She finished. "There. It's cleaned and bandaged. Feel better?"

"Much better. You're very nice." Then he added in a whisper.

"I like you very much."

She smiled. "And I like you."

Miguel continued on his way to see Clay. He proceeded to the hut that his overseer had pointed out to him. He entered and sat on a plank that rested on two coquina blocks and waited. A shorter plank resting on higher blocks served as a desk.

Life in Minorca wasn't all that great, but it was better than this place. The drought there caused a food shortage and times were hard, but at least we had real homes to sleep in. He laughed dryly to himself. All who signed on with Turnbull thought to escape hard times and find a better life. *And this is what we find.*

Clay entered the hut and interrupted his thoughts. "Chief Jacob and two slaves will go with you to get Jose Reyes tomorrow morning. If he's still alive they'll have a litter to drag him back. If he's dead, Jacob will have the slaves take him to the place we've set aside as a cemetery and bury him.

"Before you go, I have the paper for you to sign. You are no longer under the care of your parents, so we will consider you as an adult. You'll be indentured to Dr. Turnbull for the next seven years as a laborer."

He had no choice but to sign. As Clay said, Turnbull was the law here.

~ ~ * ~ ~

That evening, Miguel learned that there were still not enough huts for everyone, and some, him included, were to spend another night in the open. *It seems that I always get the worst of it. But we are lucky it hasn't rained, and cool night breezes from the river keep most of the mosquitoes away.*

The Solanos, who had a spot near his, asked about his escape into the swamp. He had become something of a hero.

"Jose and I just wanted to get back to Minorca. After we saw the conditions here, we were angry. Also, Clay was treating me like a slave."

Ramon Solano nodded. "Turnbull promised all of us that everything would be prepared for us to start planting his crops. He said the African slaves would do all the clearing."

"It's rumored that a shipload of slaves on the way here from Africa sank in rough seas," said his wife, Maria. Ramon rolled his eyes. "Yes. That rumor was probably started by Turnbull."

Maria looked at Miguel "A carpenter just came from England to supervise all the building here. He wants anybody with experience as a carpenter or mason to report to him. Maybe you can join him. Since you are..." she hesitated and her voice choked. She composed herself and continued, "...since you are on your own now, maybe Turnbull will sign you up as a carpenter."

"That would be nice," said Miguel, "but Clay has seen fit to sign me as a laborer."

Everyone was tired, and as soon as darkness began to fall they bedded down on the gray-white sand of the bank. Because of the welts on his back, Miguel had to lie face down on his blanket.

~ ~ * ~ ~

The next morning, the overseers awakened the new settlers. The cooks had prepared large pots of corn gruel for breakfast. The Minorcan cooks experimented with palmetto buds, which were plentiful, and found that they could be cooked. They called it swamp cabbage, and prepared small portions of the buds to go with the gruel.

After breakfast, Miguel led the two Africans slaves and Chief Jacob to the spot where he had left Jose. As they approached, Miguel saw the log where he had left Jose, but Jose was gone. He felt a glimmer of hope; maybe Jose had improved enough to move around. But the feeling of hope disappeared quickly when he saw movement near the water's edge.

An alligator, a fairly small one of about six or seven feet, held Jose's leg in its jaws and was dragging him toward the water. Jose wasn't struggling; his body was like a rag doll. Miguel's memory of the next few seconds was hazy.

Without thinking, he rushed toward the reptile and kicked it as hard as he could in the snout. One of the slaves joined him, and the creature retreated under the rain of blows, loudly hissing as it backed into the creek.

"That was a stupid thing to do," said Jacob, shaking his head. "If either of you slipped and fell in the water it would have had you for breakfast."

They pulled Jose away from the water's edge. There was no doubt that he was dead.

On the way back, Miguel retrieved his own bag, and Corporal Jacob confiscated the bag that had belonged to Jose.

"Maybe there's some stuff in there I can trade to the Indians."

Miguel was outraged at that remark, but with great difficulty controlled his anger and kept silent.

~ ~ * ~ ~

There were two priests in the group, Father Casanovas and Father Camps. Both were at Jose's funeral, and Father Casanovas performed the rites. There were several relatives of Jose who came on another ship. They didn't know much about Jose, except to say he was a little odd and kept to himself. No one seemed to mourn his passing--except Miguel.

After the funeral, Clay made an announcement.

"You will all be happy to know that Dr. Turnbull has sent word that he will be in the colony in a few days and talk to you."

Miguel noted the glum looks on the faces of the colonists. *Why aren't we jumping for joy and cheering?*

In the next few days, the overseers selected a dozen volunteers from among the colonists to serve as corporals, in addition to the ten African corporals already used as drivers. The corporals, all from the Italians and Greeks, had volunteered.

Miguel, like most colonists, agreed that after a few days the newly appointed corporals were already showing arrogant streaks.

Funny how some people change when they get a little authority.

Most of them were easygoing until they were selected as corporals.

Not one Minorcan had been selected as corporal, probably because the overseers didn't trust them to lean on their compatriots.

I can't blame the corporals, I guess. They are not required to do any work, and they get bigger helpings of scarce rations like peas and potatoes. They do as the overseers tell them to do because they don't want to lose their privileges. But at the same time I don't like the way they treat us.

~ ~ * ~ ~

The thatched palmetto huts had finally been completed, and now there were enough for the entire colony, which had now, due to more deaths among the colonists, dwindled down to less than twelve hundred people. The huts were spread out along the bank of the river for several miles, about 50 yards apart.

The Minorcans were unhappy with this arrangement. They were accustomed to having their dwellings close together. In their homeland, they would go out to work their farms during the day and come home to socialize in the evenings.

Miguel had vivid memories of the evenings when the villagers would assemble after supper. Even though the last three years in Minorca had been a time of severe drought, and there had been little to celebrate, the villagers would assemble, sometimes in small groups, sometimes all together.

He remembered the stories, the friendly arguments, the jokes, and sometimes the music and dancing. His father was probably the best guitar player among the villagers, and was always in demand to play for the dances.

Miguel loved to listen to the guitars and castanets and watch the dancers whirl. He smiled as he remembered an uncle who could put on a great show with his comical dancing--especially after a little too much wine. He was kind of comical-looking, being tall, skinny, and long-legged, but he was a great dancer.

Miguel's eyes grew moist as he remembered his father's laughing and joking, and going back further to when he was but a child, he could see his mother as she laughed and danced.

His father had grown morose after his mother died, but as time passed he was his back to usual ways.

25

It seems that Turnbull is determined to do everything he can to make us miserable. He is hurting himself. Minorcans will work hard for those who treat them with respect. They will not do their best for Turnbull because of the way they are treated.

Miguel was assigned one of the smaller huts with three other young men. His room mates were Antony Capo, Adrian Capella and Chico Hernandez, all single men in their twenties. But one, Antony, announced that he was engaged to be married.

"I'm going to marry Anita Usina," he said, "as soon as she is of age. Our parents arranged it, and both she and I have agreed."

Miguel didn't let his surprise and disappointment show. *I had the feeling that she was taking a liking to me. But maybe she was just feeling sorry for me...*

He became aware that Adrian was speaking.

"This is not much, but it beats sleeping in the open. At least we don't have to worry about rain now."

"The Palmetto Hotel," Chico chuckled at his own joke. "Hope it don't leak. The best news I heard today was when they told us we would have to cook our own meals now. The gruel they've been giving us is not fit for pigs."

Adrian laughed. "Guess what ingredients they're going to give us to cook. It will be corn, maybe a little salt pork, peas and potatoes. We'll end up making our own gruel. There hasn't been a supply ship in since we arrived. I heard one was on the way, but sank before it got here."

"They won't let us fish until the land is cleared," said Miguel.

"They won't let us hunt, either."

"They probably don't trust us with guns," said Adrian.

"I saw the Canova family with a gopher tortoise today," said Chico. "They say the meat is good. There's lots of them around, so maybe we could catch one."

Adrian chuckled. "Sure. If we can run fast enough."

Chico laughed at the joke, then grew serious. "I guess they might taste alright. We need something different on the menu. I hear there's lots of wild blackberries around, too."

When the rations were distributed, it was just as Adrian had predicted. Miguel had a small cooking pot in his bag, as did Adrian, and each of the four had his own bowl. They used one of the pots to make a stew from their meager rations of corn, peas, and salt pork, which they would share. They planned to look for gopher tortoises and blackberries when they had a chance.

After eating, Miguel walked to the river to wash his bowl in the salt water. He took off his shirt, rolled up his trousers and stepped into the shallow water near the edge. He used the bowl to pour water on his back. It stung a little, but felt cool to the welts.

Antony came to join him. "They whipped you?"

"They gave me forty lashes for running away."

"I heard they almost beat Rafael Segui to death for arguing with a Corporal named Silas."

"I know of Silas," said Miguel.

"I'm sorry about your beating, but I came down here because I need to have a word with you," said Antony.

Miguel was curious. "Sure, what's on your mind?"

"I heard that you were flirting with Anita."

"That's not true. She just bandaged my wound." He pointed to the bandage still on his arm.

"Well, I heard there was a little flirting as she did that. Look, she's only fourteen and I'm almost twenty, but we're planning to marry someday. She may be attracted to you because you're closer to her age. I'll forget it this time, but I'm telling you to steer clear of her."

With that, Antony walked away.

~ ~ * ~ ~

Tears rolled down the cheeks of Carmen as she spoke. "Alicia Pelicer died today. They forced her to work even though she was long into her pregnancy. She dropped in the field, and the corporal would allow no one to help her." She choked up, but recovered. "I spoke with her only yesterday. She told me that Corporal Mose tried to force her to have sex, and when she refused he beat her."

Anita hugged her mother and consoled her.

"We must find a way to get word to Turnbull about the conduct of his overseers and drivers," said Felipe. "He is scheduled to come down from St. Augustine in a few days. I'll try to get word to him"

"No, no." Carmen was now fearful. "If the overseers or corporals find you are trying to inform him of their cruelty they will beat you to death."

"But suppose Turnbull already knows," said Anita.

~ ~ * ~ ~

Around noon the following day, the overseers rounded everybody up and herded them to a central area. Turnbull stood on a wooden crate.

"I will be with you for only a short space of time today," he began. "I came aboard the supply ship, courtesy of my good friend Governor Grant, and as soon as they unload their cargo, we will set sail to return to St. Augustine. I am happy to say that more food and more provisions came on the ship. I am also happy to see that you have made tremendous progress. A large part of the land is cleared and will soon be ready for planting.

"The ship I came on brought more lumber, so Mr. Miller, my chief carpenter, will now be able to start building permanent structures. You will have, among other things, good quarters, a church, a hospital, a loading dock, and a warehouse.

"I also see that Mr. Miller has already started building a house for my family, using coquina rock and good timber.

"A squad of soldiers will arrive shortly to protect us against hostile Indians. I hope that they will not be needed.

"As soon as the land is cleared, I encourage you to start your own gardens." He smiled. "My wife, as many of you know, is from Smyrna, and she loves to do gardening.

"I will have cattle, hogs, and chickens brought in from the Carolinas, and I hope to give out baby chicks to those of you who want them." He paused.

"I'm being signaled that the ship is ready to sail, so I must bid you farewell for now."

Miguel was disappointed that no one complained to Turnbull about the cruel treatment by his overseers and corporals.

They were probably acting on Turnbull's orders anyway. And everybody probably had the same thought as I did. They feared that the corporals and overseers would take it out on anyone who complained.

~ ~ * ~ ~

That night, the rations did indeed increase, but not by much. In addition to the usual rations, they received one potato, one carrot, and a cup of flour, all to be divided between the four of them.

But they had found a small gopher tortoise that day, and feasted on gopher stew.

For the next few weeks, day in and day out, Miguel toiled at the hard labor of removing stumps and roots.

We had a lot of holidays and festivals on Minorca, and we had many days when we didn't have to work. Here, the overseers won't even let us have Sundays off. It's said that some colonists are planning an escape soon, but I doubt it. Where will they go--into the swamp to die?

August 19, 1768. Miguel learned first hand that the escape would not be by land, but by sea. Some of the colonists were sailors and knew how to handle ships. A group had surprised and overcome some of the overseers. They held a half dozen of the overseers hostage and seized a supply ship that came in to unload.

The men, mostly Italians and Greeks were rounding up people to go with them to Cuba. But Miguel, and none of the Minorcans wanted to be involved in the escape. They would hold to their end of the agreement with Turnbull and depend on him to hold his end and give them their promised freedom and plot of land. An escape attempt could jeopardize all they had sacrificed and worked so hard to get.

Besides, the whipping by Jacob was still fresh in his mind, and he was hesitant to join them. But one of the men grabbed him by the arm.

"Come on, boy. You want out of this forsaken place, don't you?"

Before he knew what had happened, he was aboard the ship with hundreds of others. But they didn't set sail right away. They decided that since they had hostages, they could take time to raid the stores in the warehouse. The supply ship was loaded with mostly building supplies such as lumber, nails, and tools, for which they had no use.

They unloaded the building materials on the ship and found more desirable stores in the warehouse. As they were loading the supplies, someone suddenly shouted.

"Rum! I've found dozens of kegs of rum."

A cheer went up and everyone came running.

The finder took a sip. "Good stuff. Probably set aside for Turnbull and his overseers." He laughed. "Well, they won't get it now."

Someone else found containers of wine. The loading stopped and turned into a drunken orgy. The escape attempt turned into a riot, with the leaders losing control. Some of the rioters ran amok, looting the warehouse and destroying goods and dumping them in the river. Some began to taunt and beat the hostages. Miguel, the only Minorcan among the rioters, was disappointed and frustrated with the behavior of the rioters.

They are not afraid because they think the hostages will keep the overseers and chiefs from pursuing us. But things could go wrong if we stay around too long. They are too cocky, and that might get us caught. And if we get caught, the overseers will have revenge.

Miguel, who had never drank anything stronger than wine, tried the rum but gagged on it. *They can have it.*

~ ~ * ~ ~

"I heard that the escapees found some rum," said Anita. "They are all getting drunk now."

"They are drunken fools," said Felipe. "The whole idea of escape was foolish, but to start drinking and partying is just stupid. I heard that some of the overseers are already on their way to St. Augustine to inform Turnbull about the escape."

"Even if they make it to Havana," said Carmen, " they have no guarantee that they will get help from the Spaniards. They are all Greeks and Italians, and the Spaniards will not feel obligated to help them. Turnbull may send an emissary to claim them as British subjects, and request the Spaniards to hold them."

"But they are not all Greeks and Italians," said Felipe. He looked at Anita. His voice was sympathetic. "I hear that the boy you befriended, Miguel Ortegas, is among the escapees."

She was too thunderstruck. for words.

Oh no. I can't believe that he would be so foolish.

~ ~ * ~ ~

After two days of, looting, destruction, drunken binges, and hangovers, the leaders finally regained control. They finished loading, released the hostages, and set sail for Cuba. As they were sailing away, Miguel sighed in relief. They were finally underway and he could stop worrying, for there was no way they could catch them now. There were rowboats and flat bottoms at the colony, but they were used only to cross the river to the island and the beach.

He had not chosen to be among the escapees, but he could do nothing about it now but accept his fate.

I have no family at the colony, but I miss Anita. She is the only person in this world that I care about now. He looked back at the colony with mixed emotions. The colony held nothing but misery for him, but he longed to be near Anita

They'll never catch us once we reach the open sea. They have no way to pursue us.

But before reaching the open sea, the ship grounded on a sand bar. The escapees set to dumping their cargo into the water to free the ship. More time was wasted.

During the confusion of throwing cargo overboard, Miguel saw his chance. He could see land from their position and he judged it near enough to swim. Perhaps if he returned voluntarily they would be easy on him. He jumped overboard.

He came up sputtering and gasping for breath, and looked up just in time to see something thrown from the ship coming straight at him. The last thing he remembered was diving under water and trying to dodge the object. He blacked out.

He came to lying on the deck of the ship. One of the men was standing over him.

"You fell overboard, boy. It's a good thing I saw you in the water after a keg hit you. I pulled you out."

"Thanks," he said. He reached up to and felt a lump just above his left ear.

I guess I'm lucky to be alive, but I will never see Anita again. I almost wish he had let me drown.

~ ~ * ~ ~

Miguel later learned that the overseers had not been idle--they had taken action. As soon as the group seized the supply ship, several overseers took two of the horses and a wagon and set out for St. Augustine to inform Turnbull. Where the travel on foot had taken three days, the wagon took less than a day.

A British frigate was anchored in St. Augustine at the disposal of Governor Grant. The governor immediately dispatched the warship, with cannons and an armed crew, to intercept the rioters.

The supply ship, now freed from the sand bar, but still overloaded with hundreds of passengers and supplies, was overtaken by the swift warship only hours away from the colony.

If the fools hadn't partied for two days they might have made it.

The frigate escorted them to St. Augustine, where they were arrested. A few of the leaders of the riot were jailed. The rest were marched, under escort by a squad of soldiers, back to New Smyrna.

As he marched for the second time along King's Road, Miguel was wondering how many lashes he would receive this time--and if he would survive them.. After his last escape, he was given but forty lashes because he had turned himself in. He heard of some workers who had received up to a hundred lashes, and heard of a few who had died from the lashings. He knew they would not go easy on him this time.

When they arrived at the colony, Miguel was surprised by a commotion in the front ranks. A group broke off and ran for the river. They grabbed several rowboats and started crossing the river. Two were killed by soldiers in the escape attempt, and the rest were eventually recaptured. One group in a rowboat made it almost to the keys before being caught weeks later.

Miguel returned to his hut, expecting a corporal to be waiting for him, but nobody was there save his room mates.

They will surely punish me tomorrow. I'd might as well be ready for it.

~ ~ * ~ ~

To Miguel's surprise, nothing happened.

The next few months were routine. About three months after the escape, he learned why none of the corporals had come for him. He overheard Carver talking to another overseer, Hill.

"Gov. Grant sent word to His Majesty in England," said Carver. "I heard from Turnbull himself that the governor requested the king's pleasure on the ring leaders. The scoundrels stole a ship, which is a crime against the Crown.

"The king decided that there was insufficient evidence against all the ringleaders but two, and decreed a pardon. The two who were not pardoned were hanged in St. Augustine."

"They should have hanged the lot of them," said Hill.

"That's my feeling, too. But the governor didn't think it proper to punish any of the rioters if most of the ring leaders were pardoned, so he pardoned everybody.

"Turnbull had no choice but to await the decisions by His Majesty and Governor Grant, and then to obey them."

Hill laughed. "Guess we wouldn't have many workers left if they'd hanged all of them. But I wouldn't want to be a worker under any of the overseers who were taken hostage."

~ ~ * ~ ~

The months passed, and many hundreds of acres of the land had been cleared. Miguel, being the son of a carpenter, knew little about farming, but from associating with the workers in the fields, who were mostly farmers, he had picked up a basic understanding of farming.

But he sometimes felt envious of the carpenters, who, along with masons, blacksmiths, and other craftsmen, were treated much better than field workers. He was beginning to regret running away into the swamp with Jose, for he felt that was the only thing preventing him from having a chance to work with Miller's construction crew.

The overseers and drivers still referred to him as "the runaway boy."

~ ~ * ~ ~

Many of the workers were dropping from malaria, yellow fever, dysentery, and exhaustion. During the first six months Miguel had seen a great many of them die, some right where they dropped in the fields. The corporals were interested only in impressing the overseers at how well they could drive the workers, and the overseers were interested only in showing results to Turnbull.

And Turnbull himself seemed interested only in proving to his backers in England that his enterprise was profitable.

Sickness and exhaustion among us don't matter to the corporals and overseers. Not even death. I wonder why Turnbull is even bothering to have a hospital built. Probably to show the visiting officials from St. Augustine.

The colonists were distressed with conditions, but were too weary, too numb, and too drained of emotion to mount a protest now. The overseers were better armed since the August uprising.

The cemetery where Jose had been the first to be buried now held well over a hundred graves.

It was late December now, and the weather was cooler, much appreciated by the workers, but there was still sickness going around.

~ ~ * ~ ~

One day Miguel was sent on an errand to the supply point by Carver, and on his way he was overjoyed when he saw Anita. He stopped.

The work in the fields and her ragged clothes had done nothing to spoil her beauty.

"Anita! It's good to see you. I haven't seen you since they moved us to the huts. I'm in the same hut with Antony and he goes to visit you sometimes." He chuckled. "But he refuses to tell where you're family is located. He thinks we're attracted to each other."

She stopped working. "It's good to see you, too, Miguel. Yes, Antony is the jealous type. He thinks I'm attracted to everybody." She blushed. "But I do like you and hope we can meet sometimes."

"But Antony says you've agreed to marry him."

"That's true, but when I agreed I was about six years old. Marrying was just a fun game to me then." She smiled. "I'm in hut number twenty."

A corporal came running toward them. "You, girl, get back to work or you'll go to the post."

She picked up her hoe and began working. "The drivers won't even let us stop for a minute," she muttered.

"Don't grumble, girl. And boy, who's your corporal, and what you doin' here?"

"Corporal Jacob. Overseer Carver sent me to get new blades for our saws."

"You better get to it, and quit playin' around with the girls."

He went to the supply point to pick up the blades. While there, he found a pencil and a scrap of paper and wrote a short note.

Anita, I want to meet sometimes, too. There is a well not far from your hut, behind hut number twenty-two. and a small oak tree is near the well. I'll hang a small leather pouch on a low branch, out of sight. We can leave notes there for each other until we can find a way to meet.

Miguel.

On the way back to his workplace, he slipped the note into her hand and kept going.

I hope she meant it when she said she wanted to meet me.

That evening, he walked the half-mile from his hut to the well. He secured the pouch to a low tree branch, making sure it was out of sight. He left a note in the pouch.

Anita, I'm sorry I caused you trouble with the corporal. I am hoping that we can find a place to meet later. There is so much sadness here, but just being near you gives me a warm, happy feeling.

My best to you, Miguel

He got back to the hut to find that the others had already eaten but had saved his ration for him. They were playing poker for bits of sea shells.

Chico greeted him. "Miguel, where have you been? It's already dark out, and we were worried about you. There are rattlesnakes around here, and walking around at night can be dangerous."

"Sorry, but I just felt a little depressed and was walking to clear my head. Anyway, it's too cold out for snakes."

"We would invite you to join the game," said Adrian, "but we've got to quit now to save our candle."

Miguel noted that Antony was eyeing him, and he saw suspicion in his eyes.

Does he suspect anything?

~ ~ * ~ ~

A week later, Miguel checked the pouch, and his heart pounded with excitement when he found a note inside.

Miguel, I'm using a blank page from my diary to write, and Mama thinks I'm making entries. Antony visited yesterday, and he asked Papa if I had gone out on any night recently. He is so jealous.

He is a nice man and I like him, but I don't want to marry him as my parents wish.

I'm glad you are happy when you are with me, because I feel happy with you, too. I hope we can find a way to see each other soon.

My warmest, Anita

Miguel knew why Antony had asked about Anita going out; he suspected that the two of them were meeting. Miguel's trips to check the pouch were sometimes spaced weeks apart. The days in the winter months were short, and it was sometimes almost dark when the workers were released. It was a long walk to the oak tree, and he didn't want to arouse the suspicion of Antony by going out too often.

If Anita and I are having such a problem exchanging notes, how will we ever expect to arrange a rendezvous?

~ ~ * ~ ~

Time passed, and the small tree with the pouch grew taller, but the leather pouch was still within reach.

Miller's construction crew was making good progress. Turnbull's house--it looked more like a mansion-- was near completion. Small frame and coquina houses were built for overseers and craftsmen and some of the colonists and their families, but still the majority of the workers lived in thatched palmetto huts. More frame houses were promised to be built later for all the remaining colonists.

A barracks for the soldiers and a warehouse was already completed. A wharf was under construction and a crew had started on the hospital promised by Turnbull.

But several of Miller's crew had come down with sickness and died. He was looking for help. He put out the word, with Turnbull's backing, that if anyone was adequately qualified as a carpenter, he would cut the term of indenture to three years.

Miguel applied, was interviewed by Miller, and accepted. However, Clay objected to Miguel's selection as a craftsman, and an argument between Miller and Clay ensued.

Miller called Miguel to his office, a cabin that also served as Miller's quarters.

"You've shown me that you're a competent carpenter, and I need you on my crew. But Clay is in charge while Turnbull is gone, and he has ordered me not to accept you.

"There's not much I can do about it. Clay is one of Turnbull's favorites, and he has a lot of influence. All I can promise, Miguel, is that I will talk to Turnbull on his next visit here."

Miguel, sorely disappointed, returned to his assigned duties with Carver. The clearing of the land was completed, and Carver was now overseeing the digging of drainage canals.

So Clay is one of Turnbull's favorites, and I am on Clay's blacklist. I might as well resign myself to laboring in the fields as long as I'm here.

~ ~ * ~ ~

The next chance that came to go to the tree, he found a note from Anita in the pouch.

Miguel, I am longing for the time when we will be together. I just turned sixteen, and Mama has said that the marriage to Antony will take place when I turn seventeen. I told Mama that I would rather wait until we are free from servitude. She agreed that might be best, and that she would think on it.

My overseer told me today that I have been selected to be a house servant for Turnbull. His house is completed, and his furniture arrived on the supply ship today. Turnbull and his family came on the same ship, and his wife will interview me.

With my love, Anita

Miguel folded the note and stuck it in his canvas bag. He would later use the blank side of the note to write his answer.

She's sixteen. I was seventeen two months ago. Lord, nearly two years in this hell. I hope that she is accepted as a house servant. It will give her a chance to get away from the sickness and death. Work in the fields is getting worse and people are dying every day.

    He thought of a young boy, who was deathly ill but forced by Corporal Louis Bruno to work in the fields. When he couldn't work, other boys were ordered to stone him. The boy died. Miguel didn't blame the boys for the stoning--they had no choice. The corporal had threatened to beat them to death if they refused.

    A man was lashed almost to death for refusing to work on a holy day. A friend of Miguel had told of how his cousin, who is thirteen, was beaten for refusing advances by Corporal Silas. Later, in the fields, she collapsed and nearly died.

    Anita, and all of us, have seen too much death and suffering.

~ ~ * ~ ~

    The next morning Miller sent for him.

"I have good news," he said. "I talked to Turnbull, and reminded him of his promise to let me choose my crew. He will back me in selecting you, and said that he will talk to Clay. Your old contract has been declared null and void by Turnbull, and I have a new one here for you to sign. "He handed the contract to Miguel. He read it and signed. In the contract, he agreed to an indenture of three years working in carpentry and construction work under supervision of the chief carpenter.

    "My crew has cabins for the married men, and a billet for the single men. Get your tools at supply, go to the billet, and see me tomorrow morning."

    Miguel picked up his bag at the hut and went to the billet. He couldn't believe it. A wooden floor. A cot and a mattress, and even a small table and stool. After living in the thatched hut, this was luxurious living.

    He had a little free time for the first time that he had been here, and strolled around the area. He walked along a stretch of the river where there were no huts, near the spot where the coquina wharf was being built.

    He found a spot where there were shrubs along the bank. He stood there for a long while, surveying the scene. From where he stood, none of the buildings or houses were visible.

At night this would be a deserted spot...if only Anita and I could arrange to meet here.

That night he drew a crude map of the secluded spot, and added a note at the bottom.

Anita, here is a place we can meet. But we must wait until an opportunity when both of us can get away, for we don't want to cause suspicion. We can leave notes in the pouch, and when the time comes that we can both get away, we can meet.

All my love, Miguel.

~ ~ * ~ ~

Miguel's first assigned job as a carpenter was in Turnbull's house affixing shutters to the windows--a job unfinished by a carpenter who had died from malaria. He considered this assignment a stroke of luck, for he knew that Anita was now here as a house servant. Instead of taking his map to the oak tree, he kept it with him in case he might see her in the house.

But although he looked for her as he worked on the windows, the day went by without a sign of her. He saw Turnbull, his wife, some of their children, and some of the servants--but he did not see Anita.

Around noon of the next day he saw her. She was carrying a basket of laundry. As she passed by the window where he was working, he called out her name in a near whisper.

She stopped, puzzled, and then she saw Miguel. She smiled, set the basket down, and ran to the window.

"Oh Miguel, It is so good to see you. I overheard Clay talking to Dr. Turnbull, and I knew you were accepted. I am so happy."

"Yes," he said. "I can't believe it. Now that we are away from the fields, and don't have corporals breathing down our necks, maybe there's a chance we can get together." He pulled the map from his pocket and handed it to her. "It's a map of a place I found, and it's not too far away for either of us. Look it over when you have time. At last we have a chance to meet and be alone." He smiled.

She returned his smile, then whispered, "I love you, Miguel."

"And I love you. Today I..."

He was interrupted by the sound of footsteps. "Go," he whispered, "they mustn't see us."

He continued working on the window as she retrieved the laundry basket. She was walking out one door as the intruder entered the other. It was Mrs. Turnbull. She smiled and greeted him then kept on her way.

He finished the windows the next day. Miller was pleased with his work on the windows, and sent him to work with a crew who was constructing a windmill that Turnbull had ordered built.

~ ~ * ~ ~

Now that both he and Anita had jobs that gave them more privileges, they were free to attend church on Sundays. He saw her every week at the church, but could not contact her.

It was several weeks later when he found a note in the pouch.

Miguel, On the third day of April the Turnbulls will have some house guests from St. Augustine. I usually go home to my parents at nights, but when guests come, the Turnbulls expect me to help with serving the guests at dinner and then clean up.

It's always after dark when dinner is finished, and they gave me a room to stay overnight when we have guests. After dinner on the third I will be free until the next morning, so it will be easy to get out of the house.

I can't wait to see you. All my love, Anita.

He turned the note over and scrawled on the blank side. It was short and simple.

I'll be there.

~ ~ * ~ ~

When the day came, he left his room shortly after dark. Making sure that no one saw him, he proceeded to the deserted spot on the river bank. A crescent moon was shining through filmy clouds, casting a dim light on the bank. As he waited, he lay on the bank gazing up at the stars and listening to a night bird somewhere in the distance. After a short while he heard her voice, just above a whisper, calling him.

"Miguel, where are you.?"

He stood up. "Over here."

They ran into each other's arms and embraced. He gently pulled her to him, they embraced, and their lips met.

"I wish it could be like this forever," she whispered.

"It will be if we wish hard enough," he said. "Papa said that our prayers are always heard."

She giggled. "If wishing and praying will make it so, then we will marry."

They lay together on the hard packed sand of the riverbank.

They snuggled up and held each other close. He had no experience with girls, except at neighborhood dances and picnics back in Minorca.

But he had never been alone with a girl, and he felt awkward as he lay there.

"I have never…lain with a girl," he managed.

"And I have never lain with a boy."

But before long their passions took over.

Afterward, they lay there for a long moment just holding each other.

"I will never marry Antony," she whispered. "I will wait for you until we are both free of Turnbull."

"We will marry," he replied. "Nothing will come between us."

"I can get away only when the Turnbulls have house guests, and that is not very often. I wanted to stay permanently in Turnbull's house, but Papa and Turnbull agreed that I would come home every night."

"At least this is much better than before," he said.

They talked for an hour or so, and then returned to their quarters.

~ ~ * ~ ~

In early 1774 the agreements of servitude for both Anita and Miguel expired . Turnbull refused to release them, as he had been refusing everyone. His excuse for not releasing the workers from their contracts was that their term of servitude would not start until the fare for transportation from Minorca to Florida was paid in full--by working it out.

A friend of Miguel, Alberto Canova, loudly protested that this was a lie, because Turnbull had promised transportation to all who signed on as his indentured servants. An overseer turned Alberto over to a corporal, who chained him to a heavy log. He was left in the hot sun for hours without water until he apologized.

Turnbull coerced the colonists to sign up for renewed agreements by telling them that they would receive no land unless they extended their term. All their rations and supplies would be cut off.

He promised that only those who agreed to renew their contract would get their promised plots of land. Whenever a worker would demand release, he or she would be sent to the whipping post.

When his term was up, Miguel was summoned by Clay.

"I have your new letter of agreement prepared. I am instructed to inform you of Dr. Turnbull's terms. He has stated that if you do not agree to three more years as a carpenter, you will be sent to work in the fields."

Miguel saw no choice but to accept.

Anita and her papa have already been extended, he as a blacksmith and she as house servant. If I'm sent to the fields or to work in the stinking indigo vats, I may never see her again.

Roberto Arnau, a stone mason who had worked with Miguel in construction , was punished for demanding release from indenture when his contract expired. After a lashing he would still not agree. But when his wife, still nursing a child, was forced to work in the fields he finally agreed to sign as a laborer for seven years .

~ ~ * ~ ~

Most of the construction was finished now, and some of the carpenters were sent to the fields whenever there was a lull in carpenter work. Miguel was among those sent to the fields, but he was still allowed to live in his billet. His term of indenture was still only three years so he did not complain.

The temporarily idled carpenters reported to Clay for their assignments in the fields. When the overseer saw Miguel, he smirked.

"Miguel, I have a nice job for you. On the days when you are required to work for me, you will tend the vats."

"Yes sir, I will do my best."

Miguel was determined to be on his best behavior. It was not in his best interests to have enemies among the overseers or corporals. Miller, a good man, was his main boss, but now there would be times, when the need for carpenters was slack, that he must deal with the overseers.

Like all the workers, Miguel hated the indigo vats. In the dye making process, the indigo plants were placed in vats of water to putrefy. The liquid became a foul smelling mess. As he stirred with the long handled paddle, the fumes arising from the liquid were almost intolerable. Cloth wrapped around his nose and mouth did little to help.

But Miguel did his assigned tasks without complaint, and Clay began to soften. He even assigned him to the crew tending livestock, a much sought-after job.

"The man you are replacing," said Clay, "got careless and allowed a group of renegade Indians to steal three of Turnbull's best cart horses. He didn't survive Silas's whip. Don't make the same mistake."

Indians sometimes entered the colony to trade venison and skins for cloth, buttons, knives, and such. The renegades had pretended to be wanting to make a trade, and tricked the stable worker jnto being off guard.

Miguel had once befriended an Indian named Chucuraha, who had warned him to watch out for the shady renegades. Chucuraha was a Timucuan who had joined the Seminoles.

"There were many Timucuans before the Spaniards came," Chucuraha told him. "They wiped us out as a people, and what few of us are left have joined the Seminoles to survive. The English take our land, but at least they don't kill us."

So far, except for some isolated attacks by renegades, the Seminoles had not been a problem for the British. Indian hatred was for the most part focused on the Spaniards.

Miguel performed so well on this job that he was given the livestock assignment each time he reported to Clay.

~ ~ * ~ ~

My dearest Miguel, yesterday I told Mama that I do not love Antony and that I would refuse to marry him. She was upset, but accepted it. But Papa said that if I had been sneaking out to be with you he would disown me. I think Antony has poisoned Papa's mind about you. He says you are trying to take advantage of me, and that you are a troublemaker and will end up on the gallows.

Things are a little better for us now. Turnbull has kept his word about letting us grow gardens. Mama has one now, and she is growing carrots, peas, beans, onions, cabbages and potatoes. But there is still not enough food for everybody, and we need clothes. Everybody is in rags now except the servants. The Turnbulls gave us pretty uniforms to wear while working.

The Turnbulls will have guests sometime next month, but I am not sure of the date. I will let you know.

All my love, Anita

Miguel read the note--she was no longer using diary pages, but the Turnbull's stationary-- then turned it over and answered on the blank side.

My dearest Anita,

I am happy that things are a little better for you. It's a little better for everybody, and not many of us are dying now. But there are still beatings. Yesterday Corporal Silas lashed Gina Casali until she was unconscious. It was for sassing him, he said. I can't wait to see you next month. I long for the time when we can be together always. When I get my land that Turnbull has promised, I will build us a house and we can get Father Camps to marry us. I am not surprised at what Antony is saying about me. He has never liked me. I hope to prove to your Papa that it is not me, but Antony who is the troublemaker.

All my love, Miguel

~ ~ * ~ ~

Anita picked up much news from working around the mansion. After a time, the Turnbulls began to regard her as a piece of furniture, barely aware that she was around when they discussed things.

"I like his wife," she told Miguel, "I sometimes help her in her garden."

She told Miguel of how Turnbull kept himself distanced from the harsh treatment of the workers and used his overseers to enforce his judgments.

"Turnbull does not seem like a cruel man," she said. "I believe he is sincere in thinking his overseers treat us well. He believes the lies that they tell him."

She recounted how his wife once remarked on the cruel treatment by the corporals, and he argued that his corporals did not punish anyone unless they deserved it. Some of the workers were malingerers and shirkers, so such methods were justified. He said that the reason he brought in the African slave drivers was because they knew how to handle shirkers.

"His friends in South Carolina who own slaves have influenced him. He sometimes compares us with his friends' slaves and sees us as his own kind of slaves."

She heard talk of how he always had to push his overseers to produce more, as he himself was being pushed by his partners and creditors. He complained of how drought conditions had hurt crop production drastically, especially his money crop, indigo. At times, Anita thought that he appeared desperate.

To add to Turnbull's troubles, Father Casanovas was trying to bring the plight of the colonists to the authorities in St. Augustine. Turnbull dealt with the problem by accusing the priest of trying to stir up another riot, and had him expelled to Europe.

Only one priest remained: Father Camps. Father Camps had also been struggling to help the colonists, but he had been less obtrusive in his efforts.

"I think that Turnbull is a little afraid of Father Camps because of his influence on the workers," Anita observed. "I heard him tell his wife that he could not expel Father Camps as he did Father Casanovas, because he was afraid that would cause another riot."

"Yes, I think it would," Miguel agreed, "All of us love Father Camps. We loved Father Casanovas, too, but Father Camps spends much of his time mingling with us and keeping our spirits up."

"The English don't like Catholics," she said. "A visitor from St. Augustine told Turnbull that some officials didn't like the idea of having a colony of Catholics in British territory. But Turnbull thinks his colonists can be easily converted, and has already brought in a British protestant to convert them. His name is Reverend McMinn."

"I've met the reverend," said Miguel. "He's a nice man, but I doubt that many Minorcans will abandon their Catholic faith. Turnbull misjudges our faith."

~~*~~

Almost nine years had passed since arriving at the colony. Miguel was now twenty-four, and had reached the end of his second contract of servitude. He felt that Turnbull would certainly not require him to sign a third agreement. So that morning, he was confident when he was invited by Turnbull himself into his office.

The fact that Turnbull was seeing him personally indicated that he would surely be released and given his land. He was already visualizing the house he would make for himself and Anita. He was politely escorted to the office by Jacob, the corporal who had once whipped him.

Miguel entered the office, which was familiar to him because he had done some work there. The rotund, round faced Turnbull was seated behind his desk. The overseer McCormick was seated on Turnbull's right. Miguel noticed a holstered pistol on his side.

Corporal Silas, who was armed with a cudgel, seated himself in an empty chair on Turnbull's left. Jacob joined Silas.

Miguel, like many Minorcans was dark and slight of build, though wiry. His ancestry possibly went back to the earliest settlers of Minorca, the Phoenicians. He chuckled inwardly; Turnbull didn't need all that protection from one small unarmed Minorcan.

"You are a good worker and have done much for the community here," said Turnbull. His double chin and heavy jowls quivered as he spoke. "But we still have much to be done, and I have prepared a new contract for you. I will see that you are excused from work on holidays and Sundays, and that you are allotted special rations."

Miguel was outraged. "I have worked hard for over eight years. I have already extended my original term by three years." Miguel raised his voice. "When I wasn't doing carpenter work, many times I worked in the smelly indigo vats with the laborers."

Turnbull sneered and shook his finger at him. "Do not raise your voice at me, or I'll have you punished. Corporal Silas is very handy with a whip, as you may have heard. One more outburst and I'll give you to him.

"You are not the only carpenter here, you know. Because of your behavior, you can now expect your term to be seven years of laboring in the fields."

Turnbull made a show of lining through parts of the contract and inking in the changes.

"Now be a good man and don't make trouble for me. Sign the papers, and you can return to work. Otherwise you might spend the day chained in the hot sun--after Silas is finished with you."

He knew that further protests would be futile, leading only to the whipping post. He apologized and signed the contract. But as he did so, he was already plotting another escape.

After signing, Turnbull instructed Jacob to escort him to Clay, with instructions to assign him to the vats, and also to move him out from his tradesman's quarters and assign him to his old quarters in the thatched hut.

~ ~ * ~ ~

Clay looked him up and down. "You were behaving yourself there for a while," he said, "and now you've got Turnbull himself mad at you. Well, I'm going to put you on the third and smelliest vat."

It was still early in the morning when Miguel started tending the vat. This was going to fit right into his escape plan. One advantage of tending the third vat was that it was so smelly. The fumes were so bad that some actually passed out, and he had heard that a few had died from inhaling the fumes.

Everyone steered clear of it, including chiefs and overseers, and the third vat wasn't easily visible from other locations.

He did not anticipate being on the vat but a very short while. He expected it would be two hours before a chief showed up to check on him, maybe more. He would simply walk off, and have a good head start before anyone noticed.

There was no reason to stay now. The colonists were no different than slaves, and Turnbull had no plans to ever set them free and give them their promised plot of land.

This time, being familiar with the terrain, he would know what to expect. He would not make the same mistakes that he and Jose had made. He would be much better prepared.

At some point, when the right opportunity came, he would return for Anita. He would leave a note for her at the oak tree before he left, and he would get his knife and hatchet from his bag.

But they may watch me close for a while to see that I am behaving. I had better wait a few days before I start.

The stench was almost unbearable, but Miguel had endured it before and could endure it for a few more days.

Adrian and Chico welcomed him back to the hut, and as expected, Antony slighted him. Chico, who had a way of joking about almost anything, greeted him.

"Welcome back to the luxurious Palmetto hotel, sir. We hope you will enjoy your stay here."

A few days passed, and after making sure the corporals and overseers weren't watching him too closely, he decided to make his move.

~ ~ * ~ ~

Miguel made his way through the piney woods after leaving a swampy area. He had been careful not to enter the main swamp as he and Jose had done. Instead, he had skirted the swamp and was now heading in an easterly direction, into the morning sun. He hoped to make it to the river before they noticed he was gone.

He waded shallow waterways and slogged through salt water marshes, places where alligators were supposed to avoid. The piney woods soon became oaks, stunted and gnarled by the sandy soil and ocean breezes. He continued eastward toward the river.

He came to the river at a point south of the wharf, near where the boats were tied. He estimated that he had been gone for about three hours. The sun was not yet high, and there was no sign of searchers. He stole a row boat and turned the prow southward. Once they discovered the missing boat, they would assume he went north, heading for St. Augustine.

He rowed for what he guessed to be about three miles, and then turned east toward the island. The river had widened, and to the east there were numerous small islands and creeks. He continued east, finally entering a narrow creek. He reached the end of the creek, found a good spot to hide the boat, and continued on foot. Once he made it to the beach, he should be fairly safe. His only worry would be the Indians.

The Indians were unpredictable. They were Lower Creeks. The Lower Creeks in Florida were breakaways from the Upper Creek nation in the Carolinas and Georgia. The Lower Creeks of Florida were now referred to as Seminoles, which means "runaway" in the Creek language.

Some of the Indians were friendly and traded with the minorcans, but many hated them because they thought the Minorcans resembled Spaniards.

The Seminoles, like the Minorcans, sometimes hunted turtle eggs on the beach. Even though Miguel had befriended one of the local Indians, who claimed to be a Timucuan, he would have to be careful. Once he made it to the beach, he would need to start making plans for his survival. His main objective now was to avoid capture by Turnbull's overseers and corporals.

There had been a few previous runaways, but all were caught. He guessed that the previous escapees had made the mistake of running straight from the colony to the beach or staying in the open., making it easy for the overseers and chiefs to find them. The runaways probably avoided the woods and swamps for fear of panthers and alligators. They were not used to such creatures, for in Minorca, there were no dangerous wild animals.

Miguel took his chances and ran to the woods and marshes. . He remembered the fate of the other runaways. They had been whipped and then chained to heavy logs all day in the hot Florida sun with no water. Some of them died.

The sun was still far from setting when Miguel reached the beach. He must now watch for hostile Seminoles, and also for search parties from the plantation. He figured that he came out on the beach at a point several miles south of the plantation, and searchers would probably not come this far. But he would be wary all the same. He was tired, sweaty, and wet, and stretched out on a sand dune to rest. The smell of salt air and the roar of the surf crashing on the shore were soothing to him.

After resting, he began to think of survival. Food would be no problem. There were clams, turtle eggs, gopher tortoises, palmetto buds, berries, and wild fruits such as persimmons. In some locations there were orange trees, planted by the Spaniards when they controlled

Florida.

For shelter, he knew how to use palmetto fronds to make a lean-to. His only tools were an all-purpose knife and a hatchet, but that should be enough.

He thought about going to St. Augustine, as he and Jose had originally planned, but it was said that Governor Grant and Turnbull were good friends. The governor would probably arrest any runaways and have them sent back to the colony.

I will just have to bide my time and wait for the right time and circumstance. Maybe it was a bad move on my part to escape, but it's done now; there's no turning back.

He smiled, raised his arms in the air, and lifted his eyes toward the sky.

At least I'm free now.

After a refreshing dip in the surf, he made his way over dunes to a wooded area of stunted live oaks. He found the area to be high and dry, ideal to construct his lean-to.

~ ~ * ~ ~

He completed the lean-to around noon of the next day. It was a crude but adequate shelter, protecting against the elements and all but the most determined wild animals. If any should break in, he would have to depend on his knife and hatchet for defense.

Next, he decided to try his hand at spear fishing. If only he had his cast net, he could easily haul in a net full of mullet. There were small ponds in the area, so he fashioned a sharp stick for spearing.

He found a small fresh water pond near his lean-to, which appeared to be formed from the cold water of an artesian spring. The pond was only knee-deep and he saw nothing but tadpoles.

He gave up spear fishing and headed for the beach to dig clams. At least he knew something about clam digging. As he was leaving the wooded area, he was startled to hear human voices behind him. He turned to see a group of Seminoles. Luckily thick brush was between him and the Indians, and they had not seen him yet.

He hit the dirt and lay still as a statue, afraid even to breathe. The Seminoles were highly skilled as hunters and warriors. They had not seen him simply because they were not actively looking for movements of any kind. They were returning from a hunt, carrying a number of carcasses of small game.

They were laughing and talking. If they were still on the hunt, or were a war party, they would be silent, using sign language.

He waited until the sound of their voices died before rising and continuing on his way. He had gone but a short way when he again heard voices. He turned to see a group of four behind him. This time the group saw him.

His instinct was to run, but the group had him surrounded before he could react. They did not look friendly. He drew his knife and hatchet from his belt, the only weapons he had, and decided he would go down fighting. They carried long, stout spears, making his weapons look ineffectual. One of the group stepped forward. Miguel sighed in relief as he recognized the man as Chucuraha, his Timucuan friend.

Chucuraha came forward and grasped his hand. "Miguel! I did not recognize you at first, my friend. I am surprised to find you here. We suspected that one lone white man not good. What are you doing away from your people?"

Miguel explained all that had happened. Chucuraha did not speak Spanish or Catalan, but spoke fair English. Miguel's English, too, was only fair, but good enough that the two could communicate.

"I will come back tomorrow morning," said the Timucuan, "and bring food, blanket and tobacco. We can talk. It is now late, and I must go."

~ ~ * ~ ~

Early the next morning, Chucuraha was true to his word. After breakfast, the two men smoked on a pipe and talked. Presently the Timucuan rose. "I must go now. It is time to help tend crops and animals. Please let me know if I can do anything to help."

"Maybe there is," replied Miguel. "Do you plan to go to the colony soon?"

"Yes, I have some skins to trade for cloth. I can go soon."

"Look for Father Camps at the church. Pretend you want to trade for some of his wine. When you are alone with him, tell him I am alive and well. Also ask him to tell Anita Usina not to worry."

Chucuraha promised and then left.

~ ~ * ~ ~

Miguel credited Father Pedro Camps for uplifting the morale of the Minorcans through all their suffering, especially the first year when so many died from malaria, dysentery, and other diseases. Their bodies, weakened by malnourishment and brutal treatment by Turnbull's corporals, had little defense against the diseases. Miguel had watched helplessly as those too sick to work were forced into the fields by the chiefs. Even children and pregnant women were not excused.

But Father Camps was there with them, lifting their spirits and giving what comfort he could. The protestant Reverend McMinn, though sympathetic, was unable to get through to any except the overseers and no more than a half-dozen of the colonists.

Father Casanovas had fought for the people, too, by trying to reach officials at a higher level. But Father Camps mingled with the workers. He had their confidence. The overseers, as well as Turnbull, were leery of him because he had the potential to whip the workers into a full scale revolt.

Apparently the overseers and corporalss had standing orders from Turnbull to allow Father Camps to come and go pretty much as he pleased.

But there was little hope for the colonists to escape from their situation. Where would they go? What would they do? They were surrounded by woods and swamps filled with hostile Indians and dangerous animals. They clung to their only hope: to serve out their indenture contracts and receive their plot of land. And Father Camps was there to give encouragement to that end. Once, when Miguel was alone with the priest, he asked why God allowed the poor Minorcans to suffer, while the overseers and drivers were comfortable. Turnbull himself lived in luxury in a mansion with house servants.

"I can only reply," said Father Camps, "that these conditions were created by men, and not by God. God gave us a perfect world in the beginning, and we are responsible for what it is today. The sun shines on the good and the bad, and it rains on the good and the bad. What we make of our lives is up to us. Of course, God does intervene at times, at his discretion.

"But we can take comfort in knowing that this life is but a tick of the clock. Those of us with faith can look forward to a far greater life after we leave this world. Only then will we see clearly and understand why all this happens."

Miguel could certainly see the truth in "What we make of our lives is up to us." He had made a mess of his own, and was beginning to regret running away. Most of all, he regretted leaving Anita.

He closed his eyes and saw her delicate features, big brown eyes, straight nose, and full lips. Once they were both free, they had planned to marry. They could work their own farm, and he could use his carpentry skills to build a decent house. But there was no turning back now, for if he did he would be whipped to death. He must bide his time and wait for the right opportunity. If he prayed, he thought, perhaps God would intervene.

~ ~ * ~ ~

Several weeks later, Chucuraha paid him another visit. He presented Miguel with a sack of corn, beans, and other vegetables. He thanked Chucuraha for the gift. "I found a gopher tortoise yesterday. I can make gopher stew with the vegetables, and you are welcome to a meal with me."

"Thank you, my friend, but I must return soon. Before I leave, I have a message for you," said the Timucuan. "It is from your shaman, Father Camps."

Miguel was surprised. "You saw him again? What did he say?"

"My chief wanted more cloth, so I went back to the plantation to trade. Father Camps took me to his church house." He smiled. "He said to tell you that Anita wishes to meet you in the secret place, ten days from tonight, but only if you can come safely."

With that Chucuraha bade farewell and left.

The secret place. He didn't think it would be taking a big chance, for he and Anita had never been discovered there. And the last place they would look for him would be under their noses.

Anyway, they probably thought him to be in a gator's belly by now

~ ~ * ~ ~

Miguel approached the plantation quietly. Clouds covered the moon making it a dark night, but he knew every nook and cranny here. He moved confidently, and finally he reached his destination.

He called softly. "Anita."

He was overwhelmed with joy when he heard her musical voice. "Miguel, my darling. I am here."

They found each other and embraced, smothering each other with kisses.

"I cried for you," she said. "I thought you were dead until Father Camps told me you were alright. Everybody thinks you are dead."

"I'm sorry," he said. His lips brushed hers. "I didn't mean to cause you grief. If I could do it again, I wouldn't run away."

Her hand caressed his cheek. "Don't regret it. Everybody rooted for you, and all are still praying for you. Of course Father Camps can't let anyone know you are alive except a trusted few, for fear that word would reach the ears of the overseers. But your escape has spurred some of us to action."

"You can't mean revolt," he said. "There are a score of soldiers here now. They are to protect against Indian renegades, but Turnbull could call on them in an uprising. And, too, the overseers and their drivers are better armed now. The workers might overpower them, as before, but it would be at a much heavier price in blood."

"No, not that kind of action. Some are thinking of going to the governor in St. Augustine to ask help. There is a new governor now, Governor Tonyn, and it's said that he is not as friendly with Turnbull as Governor Grant was. Some even say that Tonyn and Turnbull are enemies.

"Some officials from another plantation were here a few days ago. One of them made a remark that we must be too ignorant to know our rights, because if we did, we could get out of Turnbull's extended contracts."

"None of us are lawyers," said Miguel," we could not be expected to know our rights. But now that we have been told, perhaps we can petition the new governor."

"Two men have already made plans to go to St. Augustine," she told him. "Ramon Rogero and Francisco Pelicer requested permission to hunt turtle eggs on the beach tomorrow morning. Turnbull always grants such requests because he loves turtle eggs. On their way to the beach, they will steal a boat and make their escape."

If anyone can make it, those two can. Maybe this is the divine intervention Father camps mentioned.

The clouds broke up and a pale moon shone through. "I would love to stay here all night with you," he said, "but it is growing late and you must work tomorrow. We don't want to jeopardize your job in the mansion."

"Please. Can I go with you, my darling? I only want to be with you. My parents are still urging me to change my mind and marry Antony. Please take me with you."

"I wish it could be," he said, "but it is too risky. There are too many dangers; snakes and wild animals. And if Turnbull's people happen to find us, it will be more difficult for two of us to elude them. If they caught us, we both would be whipped and chained. Be patient and pray, and maybe your parents will change their mind. Now we must worry about getting the new governor's help. Let's hope it is true that he is not friends with Turnbull. Now go back before you are missed."

"I don't know when I will find another opportunity to come here," she said. "How can we meet again?"

"There won't be many opportunities, and we must accept that. I can't expect Chucuraha to be around whenever I want him. When he makes another visit to trade, I'm hoping Father Camps will contact him. We must depend on those two, and that will be chancy."

After a passionate goodbye, he watched her go until she disappeared behind a building. As he turned to leave, he heard a male voice.

"You there. What are you doing out here?"

He recognized the voice. It was Louis Bruno, a Corporal with a brutal reputation--the one who had the young boy stoned.

Anita's voice came in reply. "I couldn't sleep, and was taking a walk."

"Wait. I know you. You're the Usina girl...Anita. They say you are chummy with Miguel...you meeting him out here?"

Miguel started moving toward the sound of their voices.

"No. I don't know what you're talking about."

"I don't believe you. Good thing Turnbull has us doing night patrols. He thinks Miguel might be alive and hiding near here."

"No...no. I'm just walking because I can't sleep."

"Alright. I won't say anything about this if we can have a little fun together."

"No. Please. Let me go."

Miguel rounded the corner of the building and saw Anita struggling with Bruno. He Ran toward them, and Bruno turned when he heard the sound of his footsteps. Bruno's mouth flew open and he fumbled for the pistol on his belt. But Miguel was quicker as he lunged forward with his knife. It was over in a matter of seconds. Bruno lay still on the ground, mortally wounded by a stab in the heart.

Anita gasped, but she was not alarmed, for she had seen death many times in the fields. "What are we going to do now?"

"Go back to the mansion and forget what you have seen. I'll figure out what to do with the body."

~ ~ * ~ ~

He dragged the body to a nearby canal and dumped it. The canal was known to have alligators, and Miguel hoped the reptiles would at least mangle the body enough to hide the knife wound. Perhaps Turnbull would think his Corporal got careless and fell in. Miguel had thought of taking Bruno's pistol, but thought better of it, since it might arouse suspicion if they found him without it.

On his way back to the lean-to, he thought about the pair who planned to escape tomorrow on the pretext of hunting turtle eggs. Had his killing of Bruno caused a problem for them? As soon as Turnbull's people discovered that Bruno was missing, they would have search parties out looking for him, and maybe some of them would be on the island.

Miguel speculated on what the plan of Ramon and Francisco might be. They would be allowed to use one of the rowboats to cross the river to the island. But instead of going to the island, he guessed, the pair would head north up the river before reaching the island. He hoped to call to them if they came near enough, and perhaps accompany them on their mission. Maybe he could help in some way.

But he might be of more help to them by staying behind and creating a diversion to draw the attention of search parties away from them.

The pair would likely be discovered if search parties were out looking for Bruno. It was up to Miguel to help. He must think of something to create the diversion--even if it meant getting caught himself. Instead of turning his boat south toward his lean-to, he crossed the river. He landed and hid his boat, and then traveled on foot to a point near where boats from the colony normally crossed the river.

He found a good hiding place in the trees where he could look out across the river. There he would spend the night.

~ ~ * ~ ~

When he awoke it was still dark, but shortly thereafter dawn broke. He peeked out from his hiding place in the trees. In the gray light of dawn he saw two men in a boat, coming almost directly toward his position. The figures were a good distance away, but he knew it could only be Ramon and Francisco.

Maybe the search parties won't search the island after all.

But moments later, he watched as four more figures get into a boat and followed the pair. They were probably searchers looking for Bruno. Ramon and Francisco were aware of the four men, and so they changed plans.

Instead of turning north, they continued on across to the island. When the pair reached shore, one of the four searchers yelled for them to stop. Moments later the searchers landed. They were now near enough that Miguel could hear their voices.

"While you two are looking for turtle eggs," said one of the four, whom Miguel recognized as Silas, "keep an eye out for Louis Bruno. . He is missing."

"Yes sir, we will do that."

The corporal guffawed. "Be sure to find some turtle eggs, or the big man might have you whipped."

Ramon and Francisco had no choice now but to continue across the island toward the beach. The four searchers split up, with two heading north following the river bank and two heading south.

This is fitting right into my plans. I can help them in their escape by distracting the searchers.

Miguel, casually strolled out to the river bank as if he were not aware of the searchers. He pretended to discover them and began running. One of the searchers spotted him and shouted. All four of them immediately gave chase. Miguel had a head start of about thirty yards. He turned and ran into the scrubby oaks, which did not give much concealment.

Miguel was lean, and toughened by his stay in the wild. The drivers were given extra rations by Turnbull, and were not required to do physical labor. As a result they were soft and flabby, and Miguel easily gained on them. He saw that they were tiring and falling behind. He glanced over his shoulder to see that his pursuers had stopped.

He guessed that they intended to send one of their party back to get help, and feared that Ramon and Francisco had not had time to get back to their boat and set out yet. He pretended to stumble and fall, making sure that the men could see him. He waited a few seconds, and got up limping. The men, seeing his predicament, resumed the chase.

He had allowed the men to gain on him, so as to keep them in the chase. Suddenly a shot sounded, and a bullet kicked up dirt only inches from his heel. He had allowed them to get too close-- close enough to take aim and fire. He kept going, managing to keep trees between him and his pursuers to prevent them from getting a clean shot.

After he was confident that Ramon and Francisco had time to go upriver and get out of sight, he speeded up and lost his pursuers. He prayed that the pair would reach St. Augustine safely.

He circled back to where he had hidden his boat, and continued rowing southward toward his lean-to.

~ ~ * ~ ~

Miguel kept track of the days by carving marks on a large oak near his hideout. Fifteen days had passed since he eluded the four searchers. During that time he had heard from Chucuraha once, on the eighth day.

He learned from the Timucuan that his four pursuers had returned with a large search party. The search party blanketed a large area, but never came close to Miguel's lean-to.

He also learned that the body of Bruno had never been found. The alligators had apparently left nothing of the Corporal.

But there was also bad news: there had been no word from Ramon and Francisco.

That had been a week ago. Here on the fifteenth day it was hot and muggy. Miguel did not leave the shade of the oaks that day, and kept to his shelter. The sun was high in the sky, and he was dozing when he heard voices. He jumped up, left his lean-to, and ran to a nearby thicket, where he hid and watched for the intruders.

He watched in disbelief as Chucuraha and Father Camps arrived together. He stepped from his hiding place.

"I have good news," said the priest. "You need hide no longer. You can go back with me."

~~*~~

"Anita, can you ever forgive your foolish old papa? I was wrong about your Miguel...and about Antony, too. He told me so many lies about Miguel, and I believed him." Felipe shook his head. "Now I know that all of Miguel's troubles with Turnbull's overseers were not of his own doing, but because of the many injustices he has suffered."

"That is true," said Carmen, "only your papa and I were too blind to see the truth." She took Anita's hand. "I believed Antony's lies, too. Until now, I have always believed that he was fine young man."

"I thought he was nice, too," said Anita. "I liked him, but in the same way that I liked Uncle Alberto or Cousin Carlos." She giggled. "Or maybe like the Three Wise Men who bring gifts to the kids."

"Yes," said Felipe. "I could see the admiration you had for him when you were a young girl. But you are no longer a child. You have a mind...and heart...of your own".

He paused a moment, then went on. "When I told Antony that we must nullify the betrothal agreement because of recent developments, and that I and your mama are bound to honor the wishes of our daughter, he went into a rage, cursing and spouting unbelievably foul language."

~~*~~

Father Camps filled Miguel in on all that had happened. Ramon Rogero and Francisco Pelicer succeeded in reaching the new governor, Patrick Tonyn, in St. Augustine.

The governor dispatched a team of soldiers and officials to the New Smyrna colony to investigate. They saw first hand the disgraceful conditions of the colony: the inadequate shelter, lack of food, insufficient clothing, and emaciated condition of the people.

They interviewed and took statements from the workers and learned of the broken promises, diseases, deaths, forced labor, cruel treatment, and deplorable working conditions.

The governor ordered the release of all workers from their contracts, and granted protection to all. Father Camps pointed out that that the governor's order covered all colonists, including Miguel. All power and authority over the workers was taken from Turnbull, although he retained control of the land and colony itself.

~ ~ * ~ ~

Miguel was greeted as a hero, almost as much so as Ramon and Francisco. Those two told of how Miguel had created a diversion, allowing them to escape. Many of the people came to shake his hand: The Pacettis, Leonardis, Mastres, Andreus, Pomars, Genovars, and other friends of his father.

But most of all, Miguel was overjoyed in meeting and embracing Anita. Her parents, who had previously frowned on their affair, came forward with their best wishes for them.

Tears rolled down Carmen's cheek as she embraced her daughter. "I am so happy for you, my angel."

Felipe smiled and shook his hand. "I am thankful to you, Miguel, and am looking forward to your marriage to my daughter."

Miguel squeezed Anita's hand. "And that will happen soon after we reach St. Augustine."

~ ~ * ~ ~

Miguel was visiting with the Usinas when they received word that Turnbull was giving the Minorcans four days to vacate the colony.

"The man must be angry that the governor ordered him to give up all his work force," said Miguel, "though the governor is letting him keep the colony itself."

"He deserves to lose it all," said Anita. "He himself didn't hold the whips over us as we worked, or chain us to logs in the hot sun when we complained, or force us to work when we were sick, or work us until some of us died where we dropped.

"But he sided with his overseers and corporals when they told him we deserved such treatment for malingering. His wife sided with us, but he merely humored her as one who didn't understand how to handle workers."

The sad thing is," observed Felipe, "that if he had treated us with respect, let us hunt and fish, and did away with all his slave drivers, the colony would have thrived and been very profitable to him."

"From the way he treated us," said Carmen, "It's a wonder the colony had any success at all."

~ ~ * ~ ~

As darkness approached Miguel left the Usina's and made his way back to his old hut. Chico and Adrian assured him he would be welcome back to the hut.

Chico laughed. "When you escaped and left, the supply people were never informed, and they kept on bringing us rations for four. We're still getting your rations, so you're not mooching from us."

After supper, they went to the river to wash their bowls. As they started back to the hut, Antony caught Miguel's arm.

"Miguel, may I have a word with you in private?" He seemed to be taking pains to be polite.

Adrian and Chico left, leaving Antony and Miguel at the river bank. When they were out of earshot, Antony spoke.

"You have ruined my life, Miguel. You have stolen Anita from me and have turned her parents against me. My friends now deride me and my own parents want me to explain things to them."

"You have brought all this on yourself, Antony. I didn't steal Anita, she and I were just attracted to each other. She liked you, and saw you as a friend. Her parents liked you and had a high regard for you. You lost their trust by telling them lies about me."

Antony sputtered in anger. "I warned you to stay away from her, but you were just too damned stupid to listen. Now you're going to pay."

In their first meeting, at this same spot, it was a grown man against a boy. Miguel was not so foolish as to challenge him then. But he was a man now, though he was still the smaller of the two. Both were lean and gaunt, as were all the settlers, but Antony was taller and a little more filled out than Miguel, who had been living off the land for the past few months. But living in the wild had toughened him.

Antony charged Miguel, his fists clenched and his arms flailing.

Miguel backpedaled a few steps and moved to his left, avoiding the blows. He then counter charged with his arms pumping. He proved to be quicker, and with better reflexes. Several of his blows landed, and Antony was bleeding from his nose. He cursed, and managed to grab Miguel in a bear hug.

He pushed Miguel back and wrestled him into the water. Being bigger and heavier, he pushed Miguel's head under water and held him there.

Miguel struggled vainly to free himself, and his lungs seemed to be bursting. In desperation he kicked his knee upward. He felt it connect, and then kicked again, harder.

Antony released his hold, and Miguel scrambled out of the water. Antony was doubled over as he stood in knee deep water holding his groin.

He came out of the water and went to his knees, obviously in pain. After a moment, he cursed and drew his knife. "I'll kill you for that."

Once again he charged Miguel. Miguel backpedaled as before, and stepped aside. He ducked under a swipe of the knife, grabbing the wrist of the hand holding the weapon as he did so.

He managed to get both of his hands around the wrist, holding on with all his strength. Still grasping the wrist, he brought his knee up and once again he connected with Antony's groin. Antony dropped the knife and fell to his knees.

Miguel was now enraged. "You meant to kill me."

He began raining blows on the kneeling Antony's face until he felt someone grasping him from behind and pulling him back.

"You've punished him enough," said Chico.

Miguel turned to see that Chico and Adrian were holding him.

"Something told us that we had better come back," said Adrian, "and a good thing we did. You'd have killed him."

"Even if you had killed him, it wouldn't have been murder," said Chico. We saw him pull the knife on you."

He almost drowned me, too," said Miguel.

Antony lay on the ground moaning. His face was a bloody mess. Chico and Adrian helped him up and washed his face with river water. The four of them then started back to the hut.

Antony caused no more trouble.

~ ~ * ~ ~

The Usinas, like all the other settlers, were busy using the four days Turnbull gave them to get all their meager belongings together, harvesting whatever could be eaten and preserved from their gardens, and catching fish in the few nets available to be salted down.

Turnbull refused to give them the use of his horses and wagons to haul their belongings, but a few of the men commandeered several horses and wagons. The animals would be left in St. Augustine so Turnbull could send his Africans to pick them up.

There were no ships available, so walking the seventy-five miles on King's Highway was the only option. And so, Miguel would make the march for the third time. But this time he was in high spirits, even though he, like the other Minorcans, was weak and malnourished.

He noted that the others were in high spirits, even those worse off than he.

However, there were a few who were too sick to travel at all, and had no choice but to remain behind. Father Camps arranged with Turnbull to stay behind with them and take care of them until they either died or got healthy enough to travel.

A few others voluntarily remained behind; they were the diehards who thought that they would eventually get their promised plot of land.

They might be the smart ones, thought Miguel. *But I doubt it. It is said that Turnbull is so deep in debt that he will lose everything.*

We who are going to St Augustine have no promise of anything but a section of the city where we can stay.

But we will be free, and that is the main thing.
~ ~ * ~ ~

Epilogue

After their arrival in St. Augustine, the Minorcans still faced many hardships. There were still diseases to contend with and some deaths. But now they were left to their own devices, in control of their own fate. Tonyn granted them small plots of land in the north part of the city. Though the plots were much smaller than had been promised by Turnbull, the plots now belonged to them and were no longer just promises.

As Indian hostility decreased, the farmers were able to till land farther out from the town. Through hard work and perseverance they overcame many obstacles and eventually prospered.

Those with skills such as carpenters, potters, cobblers, masons, and blacksmiths plied their trade. The farmers among them farmed the surrounding area successfully, and the fishermen prospered in waters teeming with fish.

~ ~ * ~ ~

In 1783 Spain regained control of Florida because they had sided with the winning American colonies against the British in their war for independence. Thus ended twenty years of British rule in Florida.

The Minorcans got along well with the British in St. Augustine, but still they were glad to once again come under Spanish rule since they considered themselves to be culturally closer to the Spaniards.

When The United States, through a purchase of five million dollars, acquired Florida from Spain, the Minorcans stayed and became American citizens.

The descendants of the Minorcans who made the march from Turnbull's colony eventually became the dominant population of St. Augustine, and they were the majority of the city's populace until the last few decades of the twentieth century, when a heavy influx of people from other states moved in and settled.

Though they no longer speak Catalan, the language of their ancestors, St. Augustine natives are proud of their heritage, and still call themselves Minorcans.

They practice some traditions of Minorca and enjoy some Minorcan foods. The city has festivals honoring its Minorcan heritage.

The End

Author's Notes

"Corporal" was the term Turnbull used for his slave drivers. He purchased several African slaves from his friends who owned cotton plantations in South Carolina and brought them to Florida. He selected certain men from among his African slaves to be his corporals, giving them special treatment and privileges. The idea was to use them to motivate his workers.

Indentured servitude is a contract between a servant and master, where the servant is willingly under servitude for a set period of time in exchange for property or other payment at the end of the period. When the servant is forced to work under servitude against his or her will, it becomes slavery.

The Seminoles are not native to Florida. They were breakaways from the Creek Nation of the Carolinas and Georgia who fled to Florida and settled. "Seminole" in the Creek language means runaway. There were several nations native to Florida, including the Timucuans. Tragically, all the Florida nations were wiped out by the Spaniards, as was the Taino nation of the Caribbean.

Catalan, spoken in Minorca, is a language of Spain, spoken around the Barcelona region. There are differences in Catalan and Castillian Spanish, but speakers of the two languages can understand each other fairly well.

Dr. Turnbull managed to settle his debts, and he and his wife moved to the American colony of South Carolina. He became a respected member of the medical profession there, and lived out his life quite comfortably.

About the Author

Donald H Sullivan started his writing career while serving in the US Army. His many assignments included writing technical and field manuals, pretty dry stuff. He now writes mainly science fiction, fantasy, and horror, but also ventures into thrillers, romance, and historical fiction.. He loves dogs, so some of his stories are about those animals.

In addition to his army service, his experience also includes Federal Civil Service, insurance agent, construction worker, service station attendant, soda jerk, and delivery boy.

He is from St. Augustine, Florida.

He can be reached by email: dhsully@yahoo.com He welcomes comments from readers.

His website is at: http://www.webspawner.com/users/dsullivan

Other Books by Donald H Sullivan

Whiskers
The Psionic Man
Tales of Wonder
The Magical Earth
Our Canine Companions

The Books are available at http://stores.lulu.com/dhsully

Also available at Amazon and Bubbiesbooks.com

Made in the USA
Lexington, KY
10 February 2012